THE BOOK OF LEGENDS

THE BOOK OF LEGENDS

BY

HORACE E. SCUDDER

YESTERDAY'S CLASSICS

CHAPEL HILL, NORTH CAROLINA

This edition, first published in 2006 by Yesterday's Classics, is an unabridged republication of the work originally published by Houghton Mifflin Co. in 1900. For a complete listing of the books published by Yesterday's Classics, please visit www.yesterdaysclassics.com. Yesterday's Classics is the publishing arm of the Baldwin Project which presents the complete text of dozens of classic books for children at www.mainlesson.com under the editorship of Lisa M. Ripperton and T. A. Roth.

ISBN-10: 1-59915-030-1
ISBN-13: 978-1-59915-030-7

Yesterday's Classics
PO Box 3418
Chapel Hill, NC 27515

PREFACE

THIS little book follows the general design of *The Book of Fables* and *The Book of Folk Stories*. Literature, in one form or another, recognizes a number of stories which are current in many tongues, and may or may not have had a single origin. Such is the tale of William Tell. There are legends also which sprang up in the popular mind about some hero of real life, and, in ages which knew a marked separation between literate and illiterate, these stories, treasured by uncritical minds, came to express in supernatural terms facts and incidents which at other times would have been held fast in more exact biography. Such are the legends of "St. Christopher" and "St. George and the Dragon." Again, there are stories like "The Bell of Justice" and "The Image and the Treasure" which were the invention of mediæval preachers of a lively turn of imagination, and have found a place in such collections as *Gesta Romanorum*.

These tales, springing from various sources, have been taken up into literature of a more conscious sort, and have been made the basis of poem or story or drama. Their antiquity and their persistence mark them as corresponding to elemental conditions of human nature, and thus they have seemed to me peculiarly acceptable to the young, whose imagination is vivid and uncritical. But for the most part these stories are not accessible in a form easily apprehended by young readers, and it has been my pleasure to tell them over again in simple language. Perhaps some of the readers of this book will find a keener pleasure in after-life when they take up, for example, Longfellow's "King Robert of Sicily," or hear an opera by Wagner, because the story in each case had become familiar in childhood.

H. E. S.

CONTENTS

THE PROUD KING

THERE was once a king who ruled over many lands; he went to war, and added one country after another to his kingdom. At last he came to be emperor, and that is as much as any man can be. One night, after he was crowned emperor, he lay awake and thought about himself.

"Surely," he said, "no one can be greater than I am, on earth or in heaven."

The proud king fell asleep with these thoughts. When he awoke, the day was fair, and he looked out on the pleasant world.

"Come," he said to the men about him; "to-day we will go a-hunting."

The horses were brought, the dogs came leaping, the horns sounded, and the proud king with his courtiers rode off to the sport. They had hunted all the morning, and were now in a deep wood. In the fields the sun had beat upon their heads, and they were glad of the shade of the trees; but the proud king wished for something more. He saw a lake not far off, and he said to his men:—

"Bide ye here, while I bathe in the lake and cool myself."

Then he rode apart till he came to the shore of the lake. There he got down from his horse, laid aside his clothes, and plunged into the cool water. He swam about, and sometimes dived beneath the surface, and so was once more cool and fresh.

Now while the proud king was swimming away from the shore and diving to the bottom, there came one who had the same face and form as the king. He drew near the shore, dressed himself in the king's clothes, mounted the king's horse and rode away. So when the proud king was once more cool and fresh, and came to the place where he had left his clothes and his horse, there were no clothes to be seen, and no horse.

The proud king looked about, but saw no man. He called, but no one heard him. The air was mild, but the wood was dark, and no sunshine came through to warm him after his cool bath. He walked by the shore of the lake and cast about in his mind what he should do.

"I have it," he cried at last. "Not far from here lives a knight. It was but a few days ago that I made him a knight and gave him a castle. I will go to him, and he will be glad enough to clothe his king."

The proud king wove some reeds into a mat and bound the mat about him, and then he walked to the castle of the knight. He beat loudly at the gate of the castle and called for the porter. The porter came and stood behind the gate. He did not draw the bolt at once, but asked:—

"Who is there?"

"Open the gate," said the proud king, "and you will see who I am."

The porter opened the gate, and was amazed at what he saw.

"Who are you?" he asked.

"Wretch!" said the proud king; "I am the emperor. Go to your master. Bid him come to me with clothes. I have lost both clothes and horse."

"A pretty emperor!" the porter laughed. "The great emperor was here not an hour ago. He came with his court from a hunt. My master was with him and sat at meat with him. But stay you here. I will call my master. Oh, yes! I will show him the emperor," and the porter wagged his beard and laughed, and went within.

He came forth again with the knight and pointed at the proud king.

"There is the emperor!" he said. "Look at him! look at the great emperor!"

"Draw near," said the proud king to the knight, "and kneel to me. I gave thee this castle. I made thee knight. I give thee now a greater gift. I give thee the chance to clothe thy emperor with clothes of thine own."

"You dog!" cried the knight. "You fool! I have just ridden with the emperor, and have come back to my castle. Here!" he shouted to his servants, "beat this fellow and drive him away from the gate."

The porter looked on and laughed.

"Lay on well," he said to the other servants. "It is not every day that you can flog an emperor."

Then they beat the proud king, and drove him from the gate of the castle.

"Base knight!" said the proud king. "I gave him all he has, and this is how he repays me. I will punish him when I sit on my throne again. I will go to the duke who lives not far away. Him I have known all my days. He will know me. He will know his emperor."

So he came to the gate of the duke's great hall, and knocked three times. At the third knock the porter opened the gate, and saw before him a man clad only in a mat of reeds, and stained and bleeding.

"Go, I pray you, to the duke," said the proud king, "and bid him come to me. Say to him that the emperor stands at the gate. He has been robbed of his clothes and of his horse. Go quickly to your master."

The porter closed the gate between them, and went within to the duke.

"Your Grace," said he, "there is a madman at the gate. He is unclad and wild. He bade me come to you and tell you that he was the emperor."

"Here is a strange thing indeed," said the duke; "I will see it for myself."

4

So he went to the gate, followed by his servants, and when the porter opened it there stood the proud king. The proud king knew the duke, but the duke saw only a bruised and beaten madman.

"Do you not know me?" cried the proud king. "I am your emperor. Only this morning you were on the hunt with me. I left you that I might bathe in the lake. While I was in the water, some wretch took both my clothes and my horse, and I—I have been beaten by a base knight."

"Put him in chains," said the duke to his servants. "It is not safe to have such a man free. Give him some straw to lie on, and some bread and water."

The duke turned away and went back to his hall, where his friends sat at table.

"That was a strange thing," he said. "There was a madman at the gate, he must have been in the wood this morning, for he told me that I was on the hunt with the emperor, and so I was; and he told me that the emperor went apart to bathe in the lake, and so he did. But he said that some one stole the clothes and the horse of the emperor, yet the emperor rode back to us cool and fresh, and clothed and on his horse. And he said"—And the duke looked around on his guests.

"What did he say?"

"He said that he was the emperor."

Then the guests fell to talking and laughing, and soon forgot the strange thing. But the proud

5

king lay in a dark prison, far even from the servants of the duke. He lay on straw, and chains bound his feet.

"What is this that has come upon me?" he said. "Am I brought so low? Am I so changed that even the duke does not know me? At least there is one who will know me, let me wear what I may."

Then, by much labor, he loosed the chains that bound him, and fled in the night from the duke's prison. When the morning came, he stood at the door of his own palace. He stood there awhile; perhaps some one would open the door and let him in. But no one came, and the proud king lifted his hand and knocked; he knocked at the door of his own palace. The porter came at last and looked at him.

"Who are you?" he asked, "and what do you want?"

"Do you not know me?" cried the proud king. "I am your master. I am the king. I am the emperor. Let me pass;" and he would have thrust him aside. But the porter was a strong man; he stood in the doorway, and would not let the proud king enter.

"You my master! you the emperor! poor fool, look here!" and he held the proud king by the arm while he pointed to a hall beyond. There sat the emperor on his throne, and by his side was the queen.

"Let me go to her! she will know me," cried the proud king, and he tried to break away from the porter. The noise without was heard in the hall. The nobles came out, and last of all came the emperor and the queen. When the proud king saw these two, he could not speak. He was choked with rage and fear, and he knew not what.

"You know me!" at last he cried. "I am your lord and husband."

The queen shrank back.

"Friends," said the man who stood by her, "what shall be done to this wretch?"

"Kill him," said one.

"Put out his eyes," said another.

"Beat him," said a third.

Then they all hustled the proud king out of the palace court. Each one gave him a blow, and so he was thrust out, and the door was shut behind him.

The proud king fled, he knew not whither. He wished he were dead. By and by he came to the lake where he had bathed. He sat down on the shore. It was like a dream, but he knew he was awake, for he was cold and hungry and faint. Then he knelt on the ground and beat his breast, and said:—

"I am no emperor. I am no king. I am a poor, sinful man. Once I thought there was no one greater than I, on earth or in heaven. Now I know that I am nothing, and there is no one so poor and so mean. God forgive me for my pride."

As he said this, tears stood in his eyes. He wiped them away and rose to his feet. Close by him he saw the clothes which he had once laid aside. Near at hand was his horse, eating the soft grass. The king put on his clothes; he mounted his horse and rode to his palace. As he drew near, the door opened and servants came forth. One held his horse; another helped him dismount. The porter bowed low.

"I marvel I did not see thee pass out, my lord," he said.

The king entered, and again saw the nobles in the great hall. There stood the queen also, and by her side was the man who called himself emperor. But the queen and the nobles did not look at him; they looked at the king, and came forward to meet him.

This man also came forward, but he was clad in shining white, and not in the robes of the emperor. The king bowed his head before him.

"I am thy angel," said the man. "Thou wert proud, and made thyself to be set on high. Therefore thou hast been brought low. I have watched over thy kingdom. Now I give it back to thee, for thou art once again humble, and the humble only are fit to rule."

Then the angel disappeared. No one else heard his voice, and the nobles thought the king had bowed to them. So the king once more sat on the throne, and ruled wisely and humbly ever after.

ST. GEORGE AND THE DRAGON

In the country of Libya in Asia Minor there was a town called Silene, and near the town was a pond, and this pond was the roving place of a monster dragon. Many times had great armies been sent to slay him, but never had they been able to overcome him. Instead, he had driven them back to the walls of the city.

Whenever this dragon drew near the city walls, his breath was so full of poison that it caused the death of all who were within reach of it; and so, to save the city, it was the custom to throw each day two sheep to feed the dragon and satisfy his hunger. So it went on, until not a sheep was left, and not one could be found in the neighborhood.

Then the people took counsel, and they drew lots, and each day a man or a woman and one of their cattle were given to the dragon, so that he might not destroy the whole city. And their lot spared no one. Rich or poor, high or low, some one must each day be sacrificed to the dreadful dragon.

Now it came to pass one day that the princess herself was drawn by lot. The king was filled with

9

horror. He offered in exchange his gold, his silver, and half his realm if she might but be spared. All he could obtain was a respite of eight days, in which to mourn the fate of the girl. At the end of that time, the people came to the palace and said:—

"Why do you spare your daughter and kill your subjects? Every day we are slain by the breath of the monster." So the king knew he must part with his daughter. He dressed her in her richest apparel, and kissed her, and said:

"Ah, my dearest daughter! what an end is this! I had thought to die and leave you happy. I hoped to have invited princes to your wedding, and to have had music and dancing. I hoped to see your children, and now I must send you to the dragon."

The princess wept and clung to her father, and begged him to bless her. So he did, weeping bitterly, and she left him, and went, like those before her, to the lake where the dragon dwelt.

Now these people of Libya were heathen, but in Cappadocia, not far away, was a Christian named George, and this George was a young man of noble bearing. He heard in a vision that he was to go to Libya, and so he rode his horse toward the city, and he was hard by the lake, when he saw the princess standing alone, weeping bitterly. He asked her why she wept, and she only said:—

"Good youth, mount your horse again quickly and fly, lest you perish with me." But George said to her:—

"Do not fear. Tell me what you await, and why the vast crowd yonder are watching you."

Again she begged him to fly.

"You have a kind and noble heart, sir, I perceive," said she, "yet fly, and at once."

"Not so," said George; "I will first hear your tale."

Then she told him all.

"Be of good courage," said he. "It was for this I was sent. In the name of Jesus Christ I will defend you."

"I do not know that name, brave knight," said she. "Do not seek to die with me. It is enough that I should perish. You can neither save me nor yourself from this terrible dragon." At that moment, the dragon rose with a great bellowing from the lake. "Fly! fly!" said the trembling princess. "Fly, sir knight!"

But George, nothing daunted, made the sign of the cross, and went forward boldly to meet the dragon, commending himself to God. He raised his spear, and flung it with all his force at the neck of the monster. So surely did the spear fly that it pierced the neck and pinned the dragon to the ground.

Then he bade the princess take her girdle and pass it round the spear, and fear nothing. She did so, and the dragon rose and followed her like a docile hound. George led his horse and walked beside her, and thus they entered the city. The people began to flee when they saw the dread beast, but George stayed them.

"Fear not," said he. "This monster can no longer harm you. The Lord sent me to deliver you;" and so the multitude followed, and they came before the palace, where the king sat sorrowing. And when the king heard the mighty rejoicing, he came forth and saw his beloved daughter, safe, with the dragon at her heels.

Then George took his sword and smote off the dragon's head, and all the people hailed him as their deliverer. But George bade them give glory to the Lord; and he remained and taught them the new faith, so that the king and the princess and all the people were baptized. And when George died he was called St. George, and it fell out finally that he became the patron saint of merry England.

THE BELL OF JUSTICE

A ROMAN emperor had the ill fortune to lose his sight. He wished that his people might not be the worse for this loss; so he hung a bell in his palace, and a law was made that any one who had a wrong to be righted must pull the rope with his own hands and thus ring the bell. When the bell rang, a judge went down to hear the complaint and right the wrong.

It chanced that a serpent had its home under the end of the bell-rope. Here it brought forth its young, and one day, when the little serpents could leave the place, it led them out for fresh air. While they were gone, a toad came and took a fancy to the place. Nor would he go away when the serpent came back.

The serpent could not drive the toad out, so it coiled its tail about the bell-rope, and rang the bell of justice. Down came the judge, but saw nobody, and went back. Again the serpent rang the bell in the same way.

This time the judge looked about with care and espied the serpent and the toad. He went back to the emperor and told him what he had seen.

"It is very clear," said the emperor, "that the toad is in the wrong. Go down, drive out the toad, kill it, and let the serpent have its place again."

All this was done. Now, not many days after, as the emperor lay in his bed, the serpent came into the room, and toward the emperor's bed. The servants were about to drive the serpent away, but the emperor forbade them.

"It will do me no harm," said he; "I have been just to it. Let us see what it will do."

At that the serpent glided up the bed and laid a precious stone, which it carried in its mouth, upon the emperor's eyes. Then it slipped out of the room and no one saw it again. But no sooner had the stone lain on the eyes of the emperor than his sight was restored and he could see as well as other men.

HOW THE LAME MAN AND THE BLIND MAN HELPED EACH OTHER

A CERTAIN king made a great feast, and invited many guests to it. There was to be much eating and drinking, and every one besides was to have a present. The servants of the king gave the bidding to one and another, and in jest bade two men to the feast, one of whom was strong but stone blind, while the other had good sight but was dead lame.

"What a pity it is," said the blind man, "that we cannot go to the feast, for we should have enough to eat and drink, and a present beside. But I am blind and cannot see the way, and you are lame and cannot walk."

"Take my counsel," said the lame man, "and we can both go to the feast."

"Why, how may that be?"

"It is easily done," said the lame man. "You are strong and I can see. Let me mount your back. You can carry me, and I will show you the way."

"Well said," quoth the blind man. So he took the lame man on his back and trudged along, and both sat down at the king's feast.

KING COPHETUA AND THE BEGGAR MAID

THERE was in Africa a rich and powerful king, and his name was Cophetua. He lived in a fine palace and had gold and silver dishes on his table, and his bedstead was made of ivory, and there were weavers in the palace who were always weaving new and beautiful clothes for this rich and powerful king.

But though Cophetua had all these goods, he lacked one thing. He had no wife, and he was lonely. He was not an old man,—not at all. He was young and fair to look at; and he was, beside, not spoiled by his riches and his power. He treated every one about him kindly, and he was known throughout his kingdom as a good and generous king.

The people wished him to marry, and his old counsellors wagged their heads together and named over all the young princesses in the neighboring kingdoms. They took journeys to see the different princesses, but could not agree amongst themselves. One princess was ill-tempered; another thought of nothing but her clothes; another was silly; and then, what they disliked most, all the princesses wanted so much to marry King Cophetua that they behaved ridiculously whenever his name was mentioned.

So it was that the king, for all his riches and power, led a lonely life. But he did not sit down and mope. He went cheerfully about his daily duties, and, to tell the truth, he had seen so many foolish princesses that he came to feel a great contempt for women. Mother and sisters had he none, and in his country it was not the way for young kings to see any women but princesses and slaves.

But one day, as King Cophetua was riding out to hunt with his nobles, there stood by the wayside a blind old man, and by his side was his daughter, a young maid, in poor clothing. They were beggars, for even when a king is rich he may have beggars in his kingdom. King Cophetua was about to toss a coin into the out-stretched hand of the old man, when he caught sight of the girl's face. He stopped his horse.

"What is your name?" he asked the girl.

"Penelophon," said she. Now it sounded oddly in the ears of his nobles that she did not say, "Penelophon, your Majesty," but in fact the beggar girl did not know this was the king, and so she answered simply, and looked up into his face with her clear, trusting eyes.

King Cophetua had never seen such a face as hers. It was not only beautiful; it showed at once a beautiful soul behind it. The king forgot in a moment his disdain for women. He sprang from his horse to the ground, and took the girl's hand.

"Wilt thou love me and be my wife?" he asked, a little fear in his voice, lest she should say him nay. She looked at him and saw that he was a true man. No one ever had asked her that question before, and she answered very simply, "Yes."

"Then back to the palace," shouted King Cophetua, joyously. "There shall be no hunt to-day." Amazed were the nobles, and amazed were the people, when they heard the news, but King Cophetua wedded the beggar maid, and together they reigned over a happy people.

WILLIAM TELL

SWITZERLAND is a republic, like the United States, and the men who live among its mountains are a brave, free people. But long ago the Emperor of Austria claimed the land as a part of his empire, and sent a man named Gessler to rule the people in his stead.

Gessler was a tyrant. He wished to stand well with his master, the emperor, and he ruled the bold Swiss with a rod of iron. He had soldiers at his command, and he seemed able to do whatever he wished, but there was one thing he could not do: he could not make the proud people bow down to him when he came among them.

He was angry enough at this, and he cast about for some new way in which to make them feel his power. In those days, as now, every town had a public square called a market-place. Here the people flocked to buy and sell of each other. The men and women came down from the mountains with game and cheese and butter; they sold these things in the market, and bought goods which they could not make or grow in their mountain homes.

In the market-place of Altorf, a Swiss town, Gessler set up a tall pole, like a liberty pole. But on the top of this pole he placed his hat, and, just as in the city a gilt crown on some high point was the sign of the emperor's power, so this hat was to be the sign of Gessler's power. He bade that every Swiss man, woman, or child who passed by the pole should bow to the hat. In this way they were to show their respect for him.

From one of the mountain homes near Altorf there came into the market-place one day a tall, strong man named William Tell. He was a famous archer, for it was in the days before the mountaineers carried guns, and he was wont to shoot bears and wild goats and wolves with his bow and arrows.

He had with him his little son, and they walked across the market-place. But when they passed the pole, Tell never bent his head; he stood as straight as a mountain pine.

There were servants and spies of Gessler in the market-place, and they at once told the tyrant how Tell had defied him. Gessler commanded the Swiss to be brought before him, and he came, leading by the hand his little son.

"They tell me you shoot well," said the tyrant. "You shall not be punished. Instead you shall give me a sign of your skill. Your boy is no doubt made of the same stuff you are. Let him stand yonder a hundred paces off. Place an apple on his head, and do you stand here and pierce the apple with an arrow from your quiver."

All the people about turned pale with fear, and fathers who had their sons with them held them fast, as if Gessler meant to take them from them. But Tell looked Gessler full in the face, and drew two arrows from his quiver.

"Go yonder," he said to the lad, and he saw him led away by two servants of Gessler, who paced a hundred steps, and then placed an apple on the boy's head. They had some pity for Tell in their hearts, and so they had made the boy stand with his back to his father.

"Face this way," rang out Tell's clear voice, and the boy, quick to obey, turned and stood facing his father. He stood erect, his arms hanging straight by his side, his head held up, and the apple poised on it. He saw Tell string his bow, bend it, to try if it were true, fit the notch of the arrow into the taut cord, bring the bow slowly into place. He could see no more. He shut his eyes.

The next moment a great shout rose from the crowd. The arrow had split the apple in two and had sped beyond. The people were overjoyed, but Gessler said in a surly tone to Tell:—

"You were not so very sure of your first shot. I saw you place a second arrow in your belt."

"That was for thee, tyrant, had I missed my first shot," said Tell.

"Seize him!" cried the enraged tyrant, and his soldiers rushed forward, but the people also threw themselves upon the soldiers, and Tell, now drawing his bow again, shot the tyrant through the heart, and in the confusion that followed, taking his boy by the hand, fled quickly to the lake near by, and, loosing a boat, rowed to the other shore, and so escaped to the mountain fastness.

THE DOG GELLERT

IN the mountains of Wales there lived a prince named Llewellyn. He had a fine castle, but the most precious thing in his castle was his little child. All the servants were devoted to the child, but his most constant friend, playmate, and guardian was the great dog Gellert. He was a powerful hound, and he needed to be, for there were wolves and other wild beasts in the forest about the castle.

Llewellyn had perfect confidence in the dog Gellert, and one day when he went out hunting he told Gellert to stay at home and take care of his little master. So Gellert lay down by the side of the cradle and stretched his great paws out, as if to say: "No one shall come near my little master."

The afternoon went by, the hunt was over, and Llewellyn drew near his castle. He sounded his horn, and threw himself from his horse at the door. Gellert came bounding out, but to his horror Llewellyn saw that his mouth was dripping with blood, and there were marks of blood all about.

"O faithless hound!" he cried. "Is this the way you guard your little master?" And he drew his sword and with one blow laid the hound dead at his feet. Then he rushed into the house. Everything was in confusion. The cradle was empty, and the clothes were thrown about.

He stood still, ready to faint, when he heard a little sound. Perhaps his son still lived. He went to the cradle, and there on the floor behind it was his little boy, laughing, and pulling the hair of a great shaggy wolf that lay stretched out dead beside him.

Then the whole story was clear to him. The wolf had come in through the open door, had stolen toward the cradle, when Gellert had sprung upon the wolf, had fought with him and slain him.

O happy father! O unhappy prince! To have his child back again, and to have slain that child's faithful guardian! He could not bring the hound back to life, but he dug his grave and built above it a beautiful monument, and the place is called Beth Gellert to this day.

THE WANDERING JEW

WHEN our Saviour was passing out of Jerusalem to the place where he was to be crucified, he was made to carry the heavy cross on his shoulders. Many people followed him, and others stood in the doorways of the houses he passed, or looked out of the windows.

One of these who looked on was a shoemaker, Ahasuerus by name. He did not believe in Christ. He had been present when Pilate pronounced the sentence of death, and, knowing that Christ would be dragged past his house, he ran home and called his household to see this person, who, he said, had been deceiving the Jews.

Ahasuerus stood in the doorway, holding his little child on his arm. Presently the crowd came by and Jesus in the midst, bearing his cross. The load was heavy, and Jesus stood a moment, as if he would rest in the doorway. But the Jew, willing to gain favor with the crowd, roughly bade him go forward. Jesus obeyed, but, as he moved away, he turned and looked on the shoemaker and said:—

"I shall at last rest, but thou shalt go on till the last day."

Ahasuerus heard him. Stirred by some impulse, he knew not what, he set his child down, and followed the crowd to the place of crucifixion. There he stayed till the end. And when the people turned back, he turned back with them, and went to his house, but not to stay. He bade his wife and children farewell.

"Go on!" a voice said to him, and on that day he began his wanderings. Years afterward he came back, but Jerusalem was a heap of ruins. The city had been destroyed, and he knew that his wife and children had long since been dead.

"Go on!" he heard, and he wandered forth, begging his way from house to house, from town to town, from one country to another. He wandered from Judæa to Greece, from Greece to Rome. He grew old, and his face was like leather, but his eyes were bright, and he never lost his vigor.

He went through storms and the cold of winter, he endured the dry heat of summer, but no sickness overtook him. He joined armies that were going forth to battle, but death never came his way, though men fell by his side.

He was never seen to laugh. Now and then, some learned man would draw him into talk, not knowing who he was, and would find him familiar with great events in history. It was not as if he had learned these in books. He talked as if he himself had been present. Then the learned man would shake his head, and say to himself, "Poor man, he is mad," and only after the old wanderer had left would the thought suddenly come, "Why, that must have been the Wandering Jew."

Where is he now? No one knows. Wandering, weary, he moves from place to place. Sometimes he is driven off by the people, he looks so uncanny. When war breaks out, he says to himself, "Perhaps now at last the end of the world is coming;" but though wars have lasted a hundred years, they cease at last, and still the Wandering Jew goes on, on.

THE LEGEND OF
ST. CHRISTOPHER

THERE was a mighty man living in the land of Canaan. He was so strong and could carry such heavy loads that he was named Offero, meaning "The Bearer." In those days men born in poverty were wont to join themselves to the rich and noble and serve them; in return, they were cared for all through life by their masters.

Offero was proud of his strength, and said he would serve no one but the greatest king on earth. So he went from one country to another, until he came to one where the king was richer and more powerful than all other kings whom he had seen. Here Offero stayed, and entered the service of this great ruler.

But one day, as he stood by the king in the Palace, a minstrel sang and played. In his song, now and then, he uttered the name of Satan. Every time he did so, the king trembled and made the sign of the cross. Now Offero had never heard of Satan, and he asked the king why he trembled. At first the king made no answer.

"Tell me," said Offero, "or I will leave thee."

"I tremble," said the king, "because I fear Satan. I make the sign of the cross that he may have no power over me, for he is as wicked as he is strong."

"Dost thou fear him?" asked Offero. "Then will I leave thee and seek him, for I can serve no master who is afraid of a greater."

Thus Offero left the king and went off in search of Satan. As he was crossing a great desert, he came upon a mighty being who marched at the head of a vast army. This great one hardly looked at the giant Offero, but as he passed him he asked:—

"Whither goest thou? whom dost thou seek?"

"I seek Satan," said Offero. "I would have him for my master, for he is the mightiest being on earth."

"I am he," said Satan. "Come with me, and thy service shall be easy and pleasant."

Offero joined the army of Satan, and went marching on with it. By and by they came to a place where four roads met, and by the wayside stood a cross. When Satan saw the cross, he turned in great haste, and led his army quickly away.

"Why is this?" asked Offero. "What is this cross? and why dost thou avoid it?"

Satan gave no answer.

"Tell me," said Offero, "or I will leave thee."

Then Satan said:—

"I fear the cross because upon it Christ hung, and I fly from it, lest he destroy me."

Then Offero left Satan and went in search of Christ. After many days he came upon a holy man, and asked him, as he had asked others, where he should find Christ. The holy man began to teach him, and said to him:—

"Thou art right. Christ is the greatest king on earth and in heaven. But it is no light thing to serve him. He will lay great burdens on thee. And first thou must fast."

"I will not fast," said Offero; "for my strength makes me a good servant, and if I fast I shall be weak."

"Besides, thou must pray."

"I know not how to pray, neither will I learn," said the proud giant. Then the holy man said:—

"Wilt thou use thy strength? Find out some broad, deep river, with a swift current, so swift that men cannot cross it."

"I know such a stream," said Offero.

"Then go to it, and help those who struggle with its waters. Carry across on thy broad shoulders the weak and the little ones. This is a good work, and it may be that Christ will be pleased."

Offero was glad to be given this task. He built a hut on the bank of the river, and there he dwelt. Whenever one tried to cross the stream, Offero gave him aid. Truly, he was The Bearer, for he carried many across on his shoulders, so that not one was lost. For a staff he used a great palm-tree, which he plucked up by the roots.

Long he lived in his hut, and great was the help which he gave to travellers. At last, one night, as he was resting, he heard a voice, like that of a weak child, saying:—

"Offero, wilt thou bear me over?"

He went to the bank of the river, but he could find no one. He went back to his hut and lay down. Again he heard the same voice. This happened three times. Then he lighted a lantern, and went out to search the country about. Now he came upon a little child, who begged him:—

"Offero, Offero, bear me over to-night."

He lifted the child and placed him on his broad shoulders; he took his stout staff and began to cross the flood. But all at once the winds blew, the waves rose, and there was a roaring in his ears, as if the great ocean were let loose; the weight on his shoulders bore him down more and more, until he feared he should sink. But he held firmly to his stout staff, and at last reached the other bank, and placed his burden safely on the ground.

"What have I borne?" cried Offero. "It could not have been heavier if it had been the whole world."

Then the child answered:—

"Thou didst wish to serve me and I have chosen thee as my servant. Thou hast borne, not the whole world, but the king of the whole world, on thy shoulders. That thou mayest know who I am, fix thy staff in the earth."

Offero did so, and, lo! out of the bare palm-staff sprang leaves, and among the leaves were rich clusters of dates. Then Offero knew that it was Christ whom he had borne, and he fell down at his feet.

Offero now was in the service of Christ, and not long after he went to Samos, where the heathen were killing the Christians. A man struck him, but the giant only said:—

"I am a servant of Christ. I cannot strike thee back."

He was bound with chains and taken to Dagnus, king of Lycia. So mighty was the giant that Dagnus fainted with fear when he saw him. When Dagnus came to himself, he asked the giant:—

"Who art thou?"

"My name," he said, "was Offero, the Bearer, but now I serve Christ. I have borne him on my shoulders. For this I am now called Christ-offero, the Christ-Bearer."

Thus it was that Christopher won his name, and because he was true to his name he is called St. Christopher.

HOW THE PRINCESS WAS BEATEN IN A RACE

THERE was once a king who had a daughter, and this daughter was very fair, so that every prince in all the countries around wished to marry her. Now the princess was a very swift runner. She ran so fast that no one could overtake her.

The king was in no haste to marry off his daughter, so he gave out that no one should have her for a wife who could not beat her in a race. Any one, prince or peasant, might race with her. The first man who beat her in the race should have her for wife; but whoever raced with her and did not beat must have his head cut off.

At first there were many who tried, for a great many princes were in love with her, and men who were not princes thought they might outstrip her, and so come to be as good as princes.

The girl had fine fun. She raced with each one, and she always beat in the game; a great many heads were cut off, and at last it was hard to find any one who dared to race with her. Now there was a poor young man in the country who thought thus to himself:—

"I am poor, and have only my head to lose if I do not win the race. If I should win I should become noble, and all my family would be noble also. I think I will try."

He was a good runner, and he was also a fellow of quick wit. He heard that the princess was very fond of roses. So he gathered a fine nosegay. He also had a silken girdle made. Finally he took all his money and bought a silken bag, and placed in it a golden ball; on the ball were the words, "Who plays with me shall never tire of play."

These three things he placed in the bosom of his robe, and went and knocked at the palace gate. The porter asked him what he wished, and he said he had come to race with the princess.

The princess herself, who was only a young girl, looked out of the window and heard what was said. She saw that he was poor and meanly clad, and she looked on him with scorn.

But the king's law made no choice between rich and poor, prince and peasant. So the princess made ready to run. The king and all the court gathered to see the race, and the headsman went off to sharpen his axe.

The two had not run far, and the princess was outrunning the young man, when he drew forth his bunch of roses. He threw this so that it fell at the feet of the princess. She stopped, picked it up, and was greatly pleased with the flowers. She looked at them, smelled of them, and began to bind them in her hair. She forgot the race, when suddenly she saw the young man far ahead of her.

At once off she tore the roses, threw them from her, and ran like the wind. It was but a little while before she overtook the young man. She smote him lightly on the shoulder and said:—

"Stop, foolish boy! Do you hope to marry a princess?"

But as she sped past him, he threw before her the silken girdle. Again she stopped, and stooped to look at it. It was a beautiful girdle, and she clasped it about her waist. As she was buckling it, she saw the young man well on toward the goal.

"Wretch!" she cried, and burst into tears. Then she flung the girdle away and bounded forward. Once more she caught up with him. She seized him by the arm.

"You shall not marry me!" she said angrily, and sprang past him. She was near the goal, but the young man now let fall at her feet the silken bag. The ball of gold glittered in it, and the princess was curious to see what the plaything was. She paused for just a moment, raised the bag from the ground and took out the ball. It had letters on it, and she stood still to read them:—

"Who plays with me shall never tire of play."

"I should like to see if that is true," said the princess, and she began to play with the ball. She tossed it and tossed it, and no one can say if she would have tired, for suddenly she heard a great shout. The young man had reached the winning-post: his head was safe. He married the princess, and all his family were made noble.

ABRAHAM AND THE OLD MAN

THE patriarch Abraham sat at the door of his tent. It was evening, when he was wont to watch for any strangers who might pass by, for all such he bade enter his tent. He espied an old man coming toward him, leaning on his staff, weary with travel and bent with age, for he was a hundred years old.

Abraham rose and asked the old man to come into the tent. He washed his feet, gave him the best seat, and set meat before him. The old man ate his supper in silence, but he offered no prayer before he ate.

"Why dost thou not first worship the God of heaven?" asked Abraham.

"I worship fire only; I know no other God," said the old man.

At that Abraham was very angry and drove his guest out into the dark night. Then God called Abraham and said to him:—

"Where is that stranger who was in thy tent?"

"I thrust him out," said the patriarch, "because he did not worship Thee."

Then God answered Abraham out of heaven:—

"I have suffered him these hundred years, although he did not honor me, and couldst thou not endure him one night when he gave thee no trouble?"

Then was Abraham very sorry, and went and brought the old man back, and gave him rest and sent him on his way in the morning.

THE IMAGE AND THE TREASURE

In the city of Rome was a graven image of a man. It stood upright and held out its right hand. On the middle finger of the hand were the words STRIKE HERE. No one knew what this meant, but all thought the image held some hid treasure. Thus the image was marred by blows where one person and another had struck it to find the opening.

At last a learned man looked hard at the image to see if he could find out the secret. The sun was shining brightly. It was noon, and the shadow of the image lay upon the ground. The hand of the shadow was stretched out, and the learned man saw the shadow finger.

He marked the spot where the tip of the finger rested, and at night, when all was still, he came again. He had brought a spade with him, and he dug down at the spot he had marked. Soon he came to a trap door. He raised the door and saw some steps leading down. Then he closed the door above him and went down the steps.

He found himself in a great hall, and in the middle of the hall was a table. The table was set with dishes of gold and silver, with golden knives and cups of gold. At one end sat a king and a queen. He knew they were a king and a queen by their rich robes, and by the crowns on their heads. Fine nobles, too, sat at the table, and all about were men standing.

The wonder was, there was not a sound, and not a single person moved. The king sat still; the queen sat still; the nobles did not stir; the men were fixed. It was as if they were all of stone, and so they were; for when this learned man touched them, he found that they were stone.

He went into a room beyond. There he saw many women dressed in purple. They, too, were of stone. He went into a stable: there stood horses in the stalls, and dogs; but they had all been turned to stone. So he went about the palace, for palace it plainly was, and everywhere it was as still as death. Not a living thing was to be seen; but there were riches more than he ever dreamt of.

At last he came back to the great hall. He saw that the light which lighted the hall came from a precious stone in one corner. The light, as he gazed, fell upon a stone archer, who stood with his bow drawn, and the arrow pointed at the precious stone. On the archer's brow were the words:—

"I am what I am. My shaft is sure; least of all can the precious stone escape me."

Now the learned man thought to carry away some of the treasure. He went to the table and chose some of the golden cups. They surely would be the

41

easiest to carry. But no sooner had he hid them in his cloak than, whish! the arrow sped from the bow and struck the precious stone. In an instant the stone was shivered to bits and there was total darkness.

The learned man groped for the stairs. He could not find them. He went back and forth, but he never found the stairs. He, too, became a stone statue in the secret hall.

THE FLYING DUTCHMAN

ONCE upon a time, a Dutch ship set sail from the East Indies to return to Holland. The Dutch had rich lands in the East Indies and many a poor lad went out from Holland before the mast and landed at Java, it may be, and there settled himself and grew rich.

Such an one was a certain Diedrich, who had no father or mother living, and was left to shift for himself. And when he came to Java he was bound out to a rich planter; but he worked so hard and was so faithful that it was not long before he was free and his own master. Little by little he saved his money, and as he was very careful it was not many years before he was very rich indeed.

Now all these years Diedrich had never forgotten what a hard time he had had when he was a boy; and at last, when he was a man grown and had his large fortune, he resolved to carry out a plan which he had made. He sold his lands and houses, which he owned in Java, and all his goods, and took the money he received in bags aboard a ship which was to return to Holland.

He was the only passenger on board, but he was a friendly man, and soon he was on good terms with the captain and all the crew. One day, as the ship drew near the Cape of Good Hope, Diedrich was sitting by the captain, and they each fell to talking about their early life.

"And what," said Diedrich to the captain, "do you mean to do when you make a few more voyages, and have saved up money enough not to need to go to sea any more?"

"I know well," said the captain, as he pulled away at his pipe. "There is a little house I know by a canal just outside of Amsterdam. I mean to buy that house; and I will have a summer-house in the garden, and there I will sit all day long smoking my pipe, while my wife sits by my side and knits, and the children play in the garden."

"Then you have children?"

"That I have," said the captain, and he went on to name them, and to tell how old each one was, and how bright they all were. It was good to hear him, for he was a simple man, and cared for nothing so much as his wife and little ones.

"And what," at last the captain said to Diedrich,—"what shall you do?"

"Ah, I have no wife or children, and there is no one in all Holland who will be glad to see me come home." Then he told of what a hard time he had when he was a youngster, and at last, as the darkness grew deeper, and he sat there alone with the captain, he suddenly told him his great plan.

"I have made a great deal of money," said he, "which you know I am carrying home with me. I will tell you what I am going to do with it. There are a great many poor children in Amsterdam who have no home. I am going to build a great house and live in it, and I am going to have the biggest family of any one in Amsterdam. I shall take the poorest and the most miserable children in Amsterdam, and they shall be my sons and daughters."

"And you shall bring them out to my house," said the captain, "and your children and mine shall play together." So they talked and talked, until at last it was very late, and they went to their cabins for the night.

Now, while they were talking, the man at the wheel listened; and, as he heard of the bags of gold that Diedrich was carrying home, his evil heart began to covet the gold. As he steered the ship, and after his turn was over, he thought and thought how he could get that gold. He knew it would be impossible for him alone to seize it, and so he whispered about it to one and another of the sailors.

The crew had been got together hastily. There was not one Dutchman among them, and there was not one of the crew who had not committed some crime. They were wicked men, and, when the sailor told them of the gold that was on board, they were ready for anything.

The ship drew nearer the Cape of Good Hope, and the captain walked the deck with Diedrich, and they both talked of the Holland to which they were going, when suddenly they were seized from behind and tightly bound. At the same instant the officers of the ship, the mate and the second mate, were seized, and now the ship was in the hands of the mutinous crew.

These wicked men made short work. They threw the captain and Diedrich and the two mates, each bound hand and foot, into the sea. "Dead men tell no tales," said the man at the wheel. Then they sailed for the nearest port. But as they sailed a horrible plague broke out on board. It was a plague which made the men crave water for their burning throats, and, as they fought to get at the water-casks, they spilled all the water they had.

There they were, in the midst of the salt sea, which only to look at made them wild with thirst. Though they feared what might befall them if they made for the land, they could not stand the raging thirst, and they steered for the nearest port.

But when they came into the port, the people saw they had the plague, and they refused to let them land.

"We have great store of gold," the crew cried with their parched mouths. "Only give us water!" But the people drove them away. It was the same when they went to the next port, and the next. They turned back, away from their homeward voyage, to the ports of the East.

Then a great storm arose and they were driven far out to sea, and when the gale died down they steered again for the land. And when they drew near once more, another gale sprang up, and they were driven hither and thither. And once more they were swept far away from the shore.

That was years and years ago. But when ships make the Cape of Good Hope, and are rounding it, through the fog and mist and darkness of the night they see a ghostly ship sailing, sailing, never reaching land, always beating up against the wind. Its sails are torn, the masts are bleached, and there are pale figures moving about on deck. Then the sailors whisper to each other:—

"Look! there is the Flying Dutchman!"

THE SEVEN SLEEPERS OF EPHESUS

WHEN Decius was Emperor of Rome, he hated the Christians, and persecuted them. Now he went on his travels and came to the city of Ephesus. There he had altars built, and commanded that all the people should worship the gods of the heathen. If there were any Christians there, they must worship these idols openly or be put to death.

This caused great fright in the city, and there were some who feared to die, and they did worship the idols though they had called themselves by the name of Christian. But there were seven young men who refused to worship the idols, and remained in their houses praying and fasting. When Decius heard this, he bade them be brought before him; and because they were fair and good to look on, he gave them a little time in which to make up their minds whether they would worship the idols or be put to death.

So the seven got together, and, because they were willing to die for the faith, they sold all they had and gave the money to the poor of Ephesus, keeping only a few coins for themselves. Then, hoping to escape alive, they went secretly from the city to Mount Celion, not far away, where they found a cave, and there they hid themselves.

By and by they were hungry, and one of their number, Malchus by name, went back to the town to buy some bread. He went disguised, and when he reached Ephesus he heard every one talking of the seven Christians who had fled. The Emperor Decius was furious, and was sending soldiers in every direction to hunt for them.

At that Malchus turned back, and managed to reach the cave again without being seen. He told his comrades what he had heard, and they all fell a-weeping. But he gave them the loaves he had brought, and they all ate, and then, plucking up courage, they crept into the darkest part of the cave, and, committing themselves to God, lay down and fell asleep.

Decius was very angry that the seven young men had escaped. He called their parents, but they could tell him nothing save that the seven had sold all their goods and given them to the poor, and then had disappeared. Decius sent in every direction, but the seven could not be found. Finally he gave orders that all the caves in the neighborhood should be stopped with stones; "for," said he, "if they should chance to be hiding in any one of them, there they should stay till the end of the world." So the cavern in which the seven were hid was blocked up, but the seven sleepers within knew nothing, heard nothing, that was going on.

The Emperor Decius died, and all the people of Ephesus died, and time went on. Little by little, and sometimes by great leaps, Christianity became the religion of the empire, and in three hundred and sixty years after this time Theodosius was emperor and Christianity was the established religion.

One day a shepherd, who had his hut on the side of Mount Celion, wished to make a wall about his sheepfold, and he began drawing stone from a large pile. As he drew away one stone after another, he saw that they stopped the mouth of a cavern. At last he had drawn them all away, and the cavern was open to the light and air.

With this the seven sleepers, who had slept soundly for three hundred and sixty years, awoke. They rubbed their eyes and sat upright, and began talking over the affairs of yesterday, for they had no thought except that they had slept a night.

"What," they asked Malchus, "do you think Decius will now do?"

"He will surely hunt us down, to force us to worship the idols," said Malchus. But they all agreed they would sooner die first. Nevertheless, as the day wore on, they were hungry enough, and Malchus, taking a few coins from their little store, said he would go again to the city to buy bread, and learn what he could of the emperor's doings.

When he left the cavern he saw a heap of stones lying beside the mouth, for the shepherd had not carried all away. He was puzzled, and called his comrades to look at them. They could not any of them remember to have seen them before. Then Malchus went on his way to the city, and when he came to one of the gates he looked up and saw a cross above the gate. He was disturbed, for he thought something must ail his eyes. He went around and came to another gate, and there also he saw a cross.

"Am I in a dream?" he asked himself; but he entered the city, and made his way to a baker's shop. The city had changed. The houses looked curiously older, and there were some he did not remember to have seen before, though he had lived in Ephesus since he was a boy. But what amazed him most was to hear one and another say, as they passed him, "The Lord be with you," "May Jesus bless you." What! why, yesterday, no one dared pronounce aloud the name of the Saviour!

He entered the shop and laid a piece of money on the counter and asked for bread. The baker answered him: it was his own language, and yet it was not. The baker took up the coin and looked at it curiously. Then he looked at Malchus, and began whispering to some who stood by.

At that Malchus was sure they had discovered him, and would take him to the emperor. He begged them to let him alone. He would give them his money if only they would not take him to the emperor, and would let him go back to his friends. The baker said:—

"Not so. It is clear that you have found a treasure. Show us where it is; show us where the money is that is hidden, from which you took this piece, and we will share it with you, and then we will see that no harm comes to you." For you must know that in old times, when there were many wars, people used to hide their gold and silver in some secret place, meaning to go and dig it up again when the war was over. But often it happened that the people who hid their treasure were killed in the war, and never came back for it. So, all over the East, men were always hoping they should find these hidden treasures, which hundreds of years before had been secretly put away.

Now Malchus heard this and knew not what to say; he was amazed and he was afraid, for above all he wished not to be made known. So he held his peace. But the baker and those who stood by became angry, and they put a rope round his neck and dragged him out into the market-place. They could not hold their tongues, and soon the news spread that the young man had found a hid treasure.

A great crowd gathered in the market-place, and Malchus looked about to find some friend who would speak a good word for him. But though he scanned all the faces before him, he could not find a man or woman he ever had seen before, and it was all as if he were in a dreadful dream.

Word came to the ears of the governor of Ephesus that there was a great crowd in the market-place, and a strange man among them; and the governor and the bishop sent to have Malchus brought before them, together with the baker and the baker's men. They heard the story that the baker told, and they looked at the money. They asked Malchus where the treasure was which he had found.

"I have found no treasure," said he. "I have nothing but this coin and one or two others," which he took from his pocket.

"Where do you come from?" they asked him.

"I am a native of Ephesus," said he. "I have been away from the town but a night, and have returned to-day. I needed some bread, and I went to the shop of this man," pointing to the baker.

"If you are a native of Ephesus," said the governor, "tell us the names of your parents, and where they live." Then Malchus told their names and the street where they lived. The governor and the bishop looked at each other.

"There are no such people living in Ephesus," said the governor; "and, what is more, there is no street by that name. There was one once, many years ago, but it was long since destroyed to make room for the cathedral. And this money! why, it was coined in the reign of the Emperor Decius. Now we see plainly that you are not speaking the truth. Tell us where you found the treasure, or it shall go hard with you."

Then Malchus burst forth:—

"I implore you, in the name of God, answer me a few questions, and then I will answer yours. Where is the Emperor Decius? Is he still in Ephesus? or has he left the city?"

"My son," said the bishop, "you speak strange words. The Emperor Decius has been dead these three hundred and fifty years or more."

"I am sore perplexed," said Malchus. "But what I say is true. There are seven of us who fled from the city yesterday to escape persecution by the emperor. We went and hid ourselves in a cave on the side of Mount Celion yonder. Come with me. I will show you the cave and my comrades, if indeed I be not still in a dream."

"The hand of God is here," said the bishop to the governor. So they followed Malchus and a great crowd went with them. And when they came to the cavern, Malchus called joyfully to his comrades; and they came out, much amazed to see Malchus returned, and with him so great a multitude.

Now when the bishop and the governor saw the seven sleepers, who had thus awaked, they saw they had fresh, ruddy faces, as those who had slept well and were in perfect health. And the bishop and the governor and all the people fell down and praised God for this great wonder. Then a messenger was sent straightway for the Emperor Theodosius. When he came and heard the strange news, he too was greatly amazed, and Malchus said, speaking for the seven:—

"You behold us here whom men counted as dead, and behold we have risen from the dead. So shall it be with all those who fall asleep in Jesus. They shall rise again, as if they had passed the night in sleep, without suffering and without dreams."

And when he had said this, the seven sleepers bowed their heads, and their souls returned to their Maker. The emperor bent over them, weeping. And he would have had them enclosed in golden caskets, to be kept in the cathedral. But that night they appeared to him in a dream, and said that hitherto they had slept in the earth, and that in the earth they desired to sleep on, till God should again awaken them forever.

THE LITTLE THIEF

IN one of the beautiful cities of Italy there stood a tall marble column, and on the top of the column was a statue of bronze, which shone in the sun. It was a statue of Justice, and Justice held in one hand a pair of scales; that was to say that every deed would be weighed in the balances: and in the other hand Justice held a sword; that was to say that when a man was weighed in the balances and found wanting, Justice was ready with a sword to put him to death.

Now for many years this statue stood for the government of the city. Justice was done to every one. The law was observed by the rulers, who were fair in their dealings with men, and upright. But in course of time the rulers became evil. They no longer governed justly, and the poor did not feel that they were treated by the law as the rich were treated, and this story is meant to show it.

In one of the palaces of the city there was a poor maid-servant whom we will call Martha. She went in and out about her duty, and was a faithful little thing. Although there were many jewels and pieces of money in her lady's chamber, she never took anything, and no one thought her any other than a good, honest girl.

But one day, when she came to help her lady dress for a great ball, she could not find a pearl necklace. It had been laid on the table, her lady said, and now it was not there. Martha looked everywhere, but could not find it. It was a warm night, the window was open, and she looked out. She did not think the necklace could have been blown out, but she had looked everywhere else.

No, there was no sign of it. It had not fallen upon the stone ledge below the window. Not far away was the bronze figure of Justice, and in the darkness there was a curious sight. She could not see the stone pillar, but the bronze figure stood out against the sky as if it were flying through the air. This curious sight kept her looking, and made her forget for a moment what had happened.

"Martha!" called her lady sharply, and Martha drew her head in and turned red as she thought of what she had been doing. Her lady looked at her keenly.

"Martha," said she, suddenly, "you took the necklace. You are a little thief!"

Martha was frightened at these words. She had never been called by such a name before, and she was confused, and knew not what to say. So she looked down and said nothing. The lady was angry.

"I know you are a thief!" she said again, "a little thief!"

"I am not," cried Martha, but the lady had made up her mind to it, and, as the necklace could not be found, she was certain Martha had taken it.

Poor Martha! She had no friends now, and she could not prove she had not taken the necklace. She could only say she had not. To be sure, it was not in her little box, nor in any dress she had, nor anywhere in the little room where she slept. They only said she must have been very cunning to hide it away so carefully.

And now Martha was put in prison, and the evil judges were more afraid of displeasing the great lady of the palace than of doing an unjust deed. They tried Martha, they found her guilty, and they condemned her to be put to death.

It was a strange comment on the great bronze figure of Justice that the gallows on which Martha was to be hanged should be placed just under the figure, at the foot of the column. Yet so it was, and the day came for Martha to be hanged. The cruel judges gave her no hope.

The day came, and it was dark and lowering. It was almost as if the heavens frowned on the city. The people gathered and Martha mounted the platform on which the gallows stood. Low mutterings were heard. The skies grew black. There was a sudden blinding light and a great crash. A bolt of lightning had plunged down. For a moment the people were stunned. Poor Martha thought she had been struck.

But she had not been struck. The lightning, however, had come so near that it had struck the arm of Justice that held the scales, and down had come the scales to the ground. The scales fell, indeed, at Martha's feet, and when she could see, oh joy! there lay the gleaming necklace of pearls! It was twined in the clay of a nest!

The secret was out. A magpie had stolen the necklace from the table in the palace, had flown with it out of the window to the nest he was building in the scales in the hand of Justice. Perhaps he was working it into the nest at the very moment when Martha was looking at the bronze figure.

At any rate, justice was done at last to little Martha, though men had been unjust.

THE FAIR MELUSINA

THERE was a king who ruled over Albania, and he was very sad for his wife had died. He kept by himself, and would not be comforted; but at last his courtiers coaxed him to go a-hunting, and so dearly did he love the chase that he forgot his grief.

Now one day in the woods he was thirsty, and drew near a spring to quench his thirst. And as he drew near, he heard a sweet voice singing, and it was none other than the voice of the fairy Pressina. He was alone, and he sat long listening to her song.

That was how at first he came to know the fairy. And she was so sweet and gentle that by and by he persuaded her to be his wife. It was not a very wise thing for a fairy to wed a mortal, and Pressina promised only on condition that he should never come to see her when she had children.

The king gladly promised, and meant to keep his word; but one day, the king's son by his former wife came hastily to him, and told him that Pressina had given birth to three daughters. The king was overjoyed. He forgot his promise and flew to her chamber, where he found her bathing her three daughters.

Pressina cried bitterly that he had broken his word, and he should see her no more. She took her three daughters and disappeared. Where did she go? Why, to the Lost Island. That was so called because it was only by chance that one ever found it, and even if one found it once, he might easily lose it, and never find it again. Here she reared her children, and when they were grown, she took them every day to the top of a mountain, whence they could look down upon Albania.

"My children," she would say, "you see that distant, beautiful country. There your father lives. He is king of the land, and there you might now be living happily if he had not broken his word to me, and I could no longer live with him, for I had warned him of this, and a fairy may not break her word."

This went on year after year, and at last when they were fifteen years old, Melusina, who was the first to be born, begged her mother to tell them what was the word their father gave, and how he came to break it. And when she heard the story, she was filled with wrath, and laid a plot with her sisters for revenge upon their father.

The three maidens said nothing to Pressina, but secretly set out for Albania. As they were half fairies, they could use the fairies' charms, and this they did. They seized the king their father, and shut him up forever in the heart of a mountain. Then they went back in triumph, and told their mother what they had done.

But Pressina was not at all pleased. She did not wish the king, her husband, thus put out of the way, and she punished her children for what they had done. The other two she punished lightly, but she condemned Melusina to become, every Saturday, a serpent from her waist downward. The only escape for her was to find a husband, who would promise never to look upon her on a Saturday, and who would keep his word. So long as he was faithful, all would be well.

The fair Melusina now began to roam through the world in search of this faithful husband. She was most beautiful to behold, and had every grace to make her winsome; but it was long before she could meet the man of her search. She passed through the Black Forest, and at last came to a place known as the Fountain of the Fairies, for there were many fairies about the place; it was called also the Fountain of Thirst.

It chanced that Count Raymond strayed that way one moonlight night, and there he saw three fairies dancing, but the most beautiful of the three was the fair Melusina. She was so sweet and gentle that he fell madly in love with her, and begged her to marry him.

The fair Melusina knew that she had at last found the man for whom she had been waiting and looking. Yes, she would marry him, but on one condition only. He must never look upon her on a Saturday. And Count Raymond solemnly promised that he never would.

All went well for a while. They were happy together, but the evil that the fair Melusina had done lived on. For as each child was born into the world, it was crooked and ill to look on. Yet this did not lessen Count Raymond's love for the fair Melusina. All might still have gone well had not some one whispered to the count that it would be wise for him to see what Melusina was doing on Saturday.

He was a foolish count. He became more and more curious, and at last one Saturday he hid himself where he could see, and not be seen, and thus he watched for Melusina in her chamber.

O pity of pities! He saw her, the fair Melusina, but from the waist down she was a serpent, with silvery scales, tipped with white. He covered his eyes. It was too late, and he was seized with horror, not so much at what he had seen as at the thought of how he had broken his faith.

Perhaps he might yet have kept silence. But a great evil fell upon him. One of his sons had cruelly killed a brother, and Count Raymond was beside himself with grief. Suddenly he thought how all his children had been born crooked, and how it must have been because of some wicked thing their mother had done. And as he was thus weeping and wailing in the midst of his courtiers, the fair Melusina came in to comfort him.

When he saw her, he burst into a rage, and cried out aloud:—

"Away! out of my sight, thou hateful serpent! thou wicked woman!"

Down to the ground dropped the fair Melusina in a swoon; and when she came to herself, she looked with sad eyes on her lord. She knew, then, that her time had come, and that she could not escape her punishment. The man she had been faithful to had not kept his word.

"Farewell! farewell!" she moaned. "Alas for the misery I am in. I had hoped that thou hadst been faithful, and that I might escape my doom. It may not be. The mortal in me dies, but in my fairy life I must forever fleet about the earth as a poor lost spirit."

And at that, with a little faint cry, her body fell again, but there was a rustling in the air as the fair Melusina set forth on her lone wandering. Count Raymond and those about him saw her no more. But whenever in after years there was a new lord over the castle, the country folk said that she hovered about the Fountain of Thirst, a poor forlorn wraith.

THE BRAZEN HEAD

THERE was once a wise man named Roger Bacon. In his day the wise men were almost always members of some religious order, and Roger Bacon was of the order of Friars, and so came to be known as Friar Bacon.

It was a time when learned men were trying to do all manner of vain things. They thought to discover some wonderful draught which would make men live forever. They tried to find some means by which they could turn lead or iron into gold, and they fancied there was a kind of powder which would do this; this powder they called the Philosopher's Stone.

So they mixed all kinds of powders and liquids; they were forever at work over their charcoal fires, and as each one wished to be the great discoverer, they all worked in secret chambers and behind closed doors.

Thus they came to be thought of as workers in magic, and people looked curiously at them, and were rather afraid of them. These wise men needed servants to fetch and carry for them, and they sometimes chose servants who were dull, for they did not wish any one who was near to them to know just what they did.

Friar Bacon worked much in his cell, and he had a friend, Friar Bungey, whom he trusted. He had also a merry fellow for a servant, named Miles. Friar Bungey knew what Friar Bacon was doing, but Miles never bothered his head about his master's work.

Now Friar Bacon had a great love of England, his country. And as he read in old histories, he saw that more than once people had come across the waters and conquered England. He bethought himself how he could defend the country, and thought if he could only build a great brass wall about England he could defend it.

As he thought longer, this did not seem very possible; and then he thought if he could station a brass man here and there, here and there, at points where soldiers would land; and if he could make the brass man speak, he might defend it in this way, for anybody would be afraid who came near the coast and saw a brass man, and heard the brass man shout.

So he and Friar Bungey set to work and made a Brazen Head. They fashioned jaws, and tongue, and teeth, and all other parts of the inside of a head, and set them carefully within the Brazen Head. But though there was everything with which to speak, the Brazen Head said never a word.

They were sore perplexed; they read and they studied, but could find out nothing. So then they did what the wise men of those days did when everything else failed. They went by night into a wood, and there all by themselves they called on the Evil Spirit to come out of the darkness and tell them what they were to do.

I do not know why they should call on the Evil Spirit, and not on the Good Spirit, but that is the way the story runs. So after they had coaxed and threatened the spirit, they got this answer. They were to take six herbs, or simples as they were called, and make a hot fire and steam these simples till there was a strong fume, and this fume they were to let rise into the Brazen Head.

This they were to do, and to watch the fume steadily. Some time or other, perhaps in a month or less, the fume would work and the Brazen Head would speak, and then they would know how it was done.

So back to their cell went the two friars. They got the precious simples and steamed them, and watched the hot fumes night and day, night and day. But after about three weeks of this, they grew terribly sleepy, and though they tried to keep each other awake, it was plain that they might both be asleep when the Brazen Head should speak. That would never do; so Friar Bacon called his servant Miles.

"Miles," said he, "sit you here and watch. This Brazen Head is about to speak, but Friar Bungey and I have watched so long that we must needs sleep. We look to you to take our place. Have no fear, but the moment you hear the Head speak, on that instant come quickly and wake us."

Miles was a faithful fellow, and he promised Friar Bacon he would do as he was bid. So the two friars lay down, and in a twinkling were fast asleep. Miles now was left to himself, and to keep awake he played on a fiddle he had and began singing a song, which he made up as he went along.

So he kept awake, and by and by there was a great rumble and quaking sound, and the Brazen Head opened its mouth and spoke just two words,

TIME IS.

"Well, well," quoth Miles to himself, "that's no news. I'll not wake master for that." "Go to, old Brazen Head!" said he aloud. "Hath the great Friar Bacon worked at thee all these months, and this is all that comes of it? Time is? I'll warrant thee, old Boy:—

'Time is for some to eat,
Time is for some to sleep,
Time is for some to laugh,
Time is for some to weep.' "

So honest Miles sang to the tune of his fiddle, and made up verse upon verse, wagging his head, and laughing at that great Brazen Head. A half an hour more, and the mouth opened again, and there came forth the words,

TIME WAS.

"Sure enough," said Miles scornfully; "and d'ye think I would wake my master to tell him that great piece of news? Time was, indeed! Away with ye!

> 'Time was when thou a kettle
>> Wert filled with better matter:
> But Friar Bacon did thee spoil
>> When he thy sides did batter.' "

And so did merry Miles sing to another jolly tune.

Another half hour passed. Then there came a deep rumbling and grumbling sound, and the Brazen Head opened its mouth once more and clanged out,

TIME IS PAST,

and thereat it fell over on its face and brake all to bits. And there was a terrible noise, and there were great flashes of fire, so that poor Miles was half dead with fear. He dropped his fiddle and fell on his knees, and the room was full of smoke.

Now the noise and the smoke were so horrible that Friar Bacon and Friar Bungey suddenly waked. They rushed into the cell, and there they saw Miles beating his breast and crying out, and on the floor lay the Brazen Head all in bits.

"What is this! what is this!" cried Friar Bacon. "What hast thou done?"

"Sure, it fell down all of itself!" shouted Miles.

"And did he not speak? Did he say nothing?"

"Nothing at all, at all," quoth Miles, "but just some senseless words. A parrot could say more."

"Out upon you!" said Friar Bacon, lifting his hand to strike the wretch. "If you had called us when it spake, we should all have been great men, for we should have done that which would have saved England from all her foes. What did the Brazen Head say?"

"It just said, 'Time is,' the first time," quoth Miles.

"Ah," said Friar Bacon, "you have undone us. Had you called us then, we should have been in time. Did it speak again?"

"Ay, sir, that it did, half an hour afterward, and it just said, 'Time was.'"

"Woe, woe! if thou hadst but called us then," said Friar Bungey, shaking his head.

"Sure, sir," said Miles, "I thought it would be telling some long tale, and then I would have waked ye, but it kept quiet for half an hour, and then it blabbed out, 'Time is past,' and fell down head first, and there was such a clatter that I had no need to wake ye. The old beast would have waked the dead."

Then Friar Bacon was wroth, and would have let his hand fall heavy upon poor Miles, but Friar

Bungey told him it was a shame to strike such an ignorant man. So Friar Bacon withheld his hand, but he made Miles dumb for the space of a month, in punishment, though to be sure there was not much that Miles had to say.

So nothing came of the Brazen Head, and England had to content herself with live men to guard her gates.

THE MONK AND THE BIRD

THERE was an old monk who had led a holy life, doing good all his days. And one reason why he had done good was because he lived much with God.

Early in the morning, before others had risen, he was on his knees praying to the Father of all, giving thanks for all his mercies, and asking for grace to lead a holy life that day. And late at night, when others slept, he lingered long on his knees, talking with God as with his dearest friend.

Not only did this monk pray in the chapel, and by the side of his narrow bed, but as he walked about doing good deeds his lips moved, and he scarcely saw any one else, for he was praying in silence. He was always glad to escape from himself to the thought of God.

So when he was an old, old man, he was one day in the garden of the monastery. He was too old and feeble now to go away amongst the poor and sick; but the poor and sick, young and old, were glad when they could come to him, and receive his blessing.

It was a lovely morning hour in early summer, and the garden was sweet with odors of roses. The air was soft and still. The old monk had been helped out to a garden-bench, and there left. He was in perfect peace, and when he was alone he sank upon his knees by the bench, and lifted his peaceful soul in prayer and praise.

As he prayed there came a sweet, pure note to his ear. It did not disturb him. He knew it for the voice of one of God's happy creatures, and as he prayed, he listened with a smile to this bird singing in one of the rose trees in the garden. He thought he never had heard anything so liquid as the song of this bird.

The notes so filled his soul that he rose from his knees to listen to the song. He rested his hands on his stout stick and listened. Then he drew near the rose tree from which the song came.

As he drew near, the little bird continued singing and then fled to a grove farther away, and again began calling with its sweet note. The old monk, forgetting everything else, eagerly pressed forward. It was as if he heard some bird of God.

O rapture! he neared the bird again and heard the pure notes sounding clearer and clearer. Once more the bird filled his soul and he listened, listened. Then away flew the bird, and led him by its song to a farther grove. Still the old man pressed on.

Thus hour by hour the heavenly bird sang, and hour by hour the old monk listened intent. He would not lose a note. But at last the bird's song grew gentler, until it ceased altogether. The day was nearing its close.

Then the happy old man set his face west-ward, and made his way back toward the monastery, carrying the memory of the song which mingled with his prayer, so that he scarce knew whether he were praying or listening to the music.

It was nightfall when he found himself once again within the garden; but it was not yet dark, and in the evening light he looked about him at the old scene. He was perplexed at the appearance of things. There was the convent, there was the garden, and yet nothing looked quite as when he had left the place.

As he stood wondering, a brother monk drew near. He wore the familiar dress, yet his face seemed strange. Well as our old monk knew all the brethren, this newcomer he could not remember ever to have seen. But he must needs speak to him, and he asked:—

"What has happened? Why is it that every-thing looks so changed since morning? What has taken place? But perhaps you have only just come. Is Brother Andrew within?"

The monk looked at him as he spoke, and he wondered as he looked. "Why," said he, "there has been no change here to-day, no, nor for many years. I have myself been here ten years come Michaelmas. There is no Brother Andrew amongst us. But you? pray, who art thou? and whence camest thou? This is the dress of the order, though somewhat old, but I have never seen thee before? What is thy name, good brother?"

The old monk, much wondering, told his name, and said further: "It was only this morning, early this morning, that I left the garden, for I heard the song of a bird, and it was like a song let down from heaven to draw me up."

Now when the younger monk heard the name, he fell on his knees, and took the robe of the other in his hand, and bowed over it. Then he told him how it was written in the books of the monastery that a holy man of that name had strangely disappeared out of their sight two hundred years ago.

"And it was written," he said, "that like as the Lord God buried his servant Moses and no man knew where he was buried, so did he hide from our sight this holy brother."

At that, a smile spread over the face of the old monk, and he lifted up his voice and said: "My hour of death is come. Blessed be the name of the Lord for all his mercies to me," and so he breathed out his spirit.

Then all the monks in the monastery were called to witness this strange sight; and the young monk who had held converse with the old man turned to his brethren and said:—

"God be merciful to me a sinner! When this old man drew near to me I was thinking to myself, how can I bear the thought of an eternity of happiness? shall I not weary of endless peace? but lo! our brother heard a bird of God for but a single day as he thought, and it was two hundred years. Surely a thousand years in His sight are but as yesterday, and as a day that is past."